THIS WALKER BOOK BELONGS TO:

for Rowan and Benjamin with love

First published 1991
by Walker Books Ltd, 87 Vauxhall Walk
London SE11 5HJ

This edition published 1994

2 4 6 8 10 9 7 5 3 1

Printed in Hong Kong

British Library Cataloguing in Publication Data
A catalogue record for this book is
available from the British Library.

ISBN 0-7445-3610-3

NEW BIG SISTER

Debi Gliori

WALKER BOOKS
LONDON

I heard Mum being sick in the
bathroom this morning.

I think Dad's got it too, because when I
told him about Mum, he looked a bit
ill. It's odd, though –

Mum went to the doctor about being
sick, but when she came out, the
doctor was smiling.

Dad's better now,

but Mum's off her food.

I asked Sophie if her mum was sick in
the mornings, and she said only
when she was having a baby.

I wonder what it's like having a baby.

I asked Mum at tea time. She told me
she *is* having a baby.

We all got so excited that we let the
toast burn.

Mum took a long time to grow a baby.
I had a birthday...

and our cat had four kittens, and we all
had Christmas!

Mum started to grow so big she
couldn't see her toes any more.

She ate millions of marmalade and cold spaghetti sandwiches.

One night I woke up because I could
hear Mum and Dad moving around.

When they went to the hospital to have
the baby, Grandma stayed with me.

Next day Dad came home with a big
smile on his face.

He said Mum was fine and we'd go to the
hospital after supper. He was so
tired he fell asleep over his plate.

When we got to the hospital, we went
up in the lift to Mum's room.

She was sitting up in bed and she
looked very small.

In came the nurse with a baby.
"Here's your baby sister," she said.
The door opened again and ...

in came the doctor with another baby.
"And here's your baby brother," he said.

Dad opened a bottle of very noisy
champagne and turned to me.
"To a new big sister," he said.
I got bubbles up my nose.

MORE WALKER PAPERBACKS
For You to Enjoy

Also by Debi Gliori

MY LITTLE BROTHER

Sometimes the little girl in this delightful story wishes her
bothersome little brother would just disappear – until,
one night, he does!

0-7445-3612-X   £3.99

NEW BIG HOUSE

The hall is full of baby walkers, the kitchen is bursting with
laundry and the living room is a Lego minefield… What the family in
this lively book needs is a new big house. But finding one
proves to be a big headache!

0-7445-3609-X   £3.99

WHEN I'M BIG

by Debi Gliori

A small child ponders the advantages of being big.

"Interprets every child's fears and ambitions… Debi Gliori's
illustrations are full of humorous detail which will find a wide audience
among three and four year olds." *Valerie Bierman, The Scotsman*

0-7445-3125-X   £3.99